AVALON HIGH
CORONATION

Books by
MEG CABOT

ALL-AMERICAN GIRL

READY OR NOT: AN ALL-AMERICAN GIRL NOVEL

TEEN IDOL

AVALON HIGH

HOW TO BE POPULAR

PANTS ON FIRE

JINX

NICOLA AND THE VISCOUNT

VICTORIA AND THE ROGUE

THE BOY NEXT DOOR

BOY MEETS GIRL

EVERY BOY'S GOT ONE

SIZE 12 IS NOT FAT

SIZE 14 IS NOT FAT EITHER

BIG BONED

QUEEN OF BABBLE

QUEEN OF BABBLE IN THE BIG CITY

QUEEN OF BABBLE GETS HITCHED

The Mediator Books:

THE MEDIATOR 1: SHADOWLAND

THE MEDIATOR 2: NINTH KEY

THE MEDIATOR 3: REUNION

THE MEDIATOR 4: DARKEST HOUR

THE MEDIATOR 5: HAUNTED

THE MEDIATOR 6: TWILIGHT

The 1-800-Where-R-You Books:

WHEN LIGHTNING STRIKES

CODE NAME CASSANDRA

SAFE HOUSE

SANCTUARY

MISSING YOU

AVALON HIGH
CORONATION

VOLUME 3:
HUNTER'S MOON

CREATED AND WRITTEN BY
MEG CABOT

ILLUSTRATED BY
JINKY CORONADO
& LARRY TUAZON

HAMBURG // LONDON // LOS ANGELES // TOKYO

HARPER
An Imprint of HarperCollinsPublishers

Avalon High: Coronation vol. 3
Created and Written by Meg Cabot
Illustrated by Jinky Coronado & Larry Tuazon

Layout & Lettering - Michael Paolilli
Cover Design - Chelsea Windlinger

Editor - Jenna Winterberg
Print Production Manager - Lucas Rivera
Managing Editor - Vy Nguyen
Senior Designer - Louis Csontos
Associate Publisher - Marco F. Pavia
President and C.O.O. - John Parker
C.E.O. and Chief Creative Officer - Stu Levy

A ⊚ TOKYOPOP® Manga

TOKYOPOP and ⊚ are trademarks or registered trademarks of TOKYOPOP Inc.

TOKYOPOP Inc.
5900 Wilshire Blvd. Suite 2000
Los Angeles, CA 90036

E-mail: info@TOKYOPOP.com
Come visit us online at www.TOKYOPOP.com

Library of Congress catalog card number: 2009920736
ISBN 978-0-06-117710-1

09 10 11 12 13   LP/BVG   10 9 8 7 6 5 4 3 2
❖
First Edition

For Kari Sutherland, with many thanks for

all her hard work and dedication

CHAPTER ONE

ONCE UPON A TIME, THERE LIVED A KING WHOSE DESTINY WAS TO LEAD HIS PEOPLE OUT OF THE DARK AGES AND INTO A NEW ERA OF ENLIGHTENMENT.

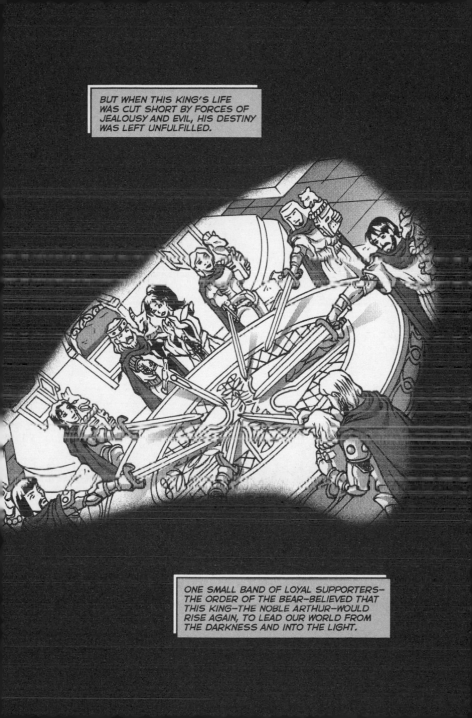

BUT WHEN THIS KING'S LIFE WAS CUT SHORT BY FORCES OF JEALOUSY AND EVIL, HIS DESTINY WAS LEFT UNFULFILLED.

ONE SMALL BAND OF LOYAL SUPPORTERS—THE ORDER OF THE BEAR—BELIEVED THAT THIS KING—THE NOBLE ARTHUR—WOULD RISE AGAIN, TO LEAD OUR WORLD FROM THE DARKNESS AND INTO THE LIGHT.

FOR NEARLY FIFTEEN HUNDRED YEARS THESE BELIEVERS HAVE WAITED AND WATCHED FOR HIS RETURN.

WILL'S HALF BROTHER, MARCO, BELIEVES IT TOO, AND TRIED TO KILL BOTH WILL AND ME. LUCKILY, HE WAS ARRESTED. BUT MR. MORTON THINKS WE'RE ALL STILL IN DANGER. BECAUSE IF WILL DOESN'T BELIEVE IT HIMSELF BY THE NIGHT OF HOMECOMING . . .

LIKE, WILL'S DAD KICKED HIM OUT OF THE HOUSE SO NOW HE LIVES WITH MY FAMILY. IT STILL BOTHERS HIM, BUT WHEN I TRIED TO ARRANGE A DINNER WITH HIS PARENTS TO SMOOTH THINGS OVER, MARCO SHOWED UP TOO. YEAH, THEY LET HIM OUT, AND ALTHOUGH HE CLAIMS HE WANTS TO BE FRIENDS, WILL STILL WARNED HIM TO STAY AWAY FROM US. NOT THAT I BLAME HIM.

CHAPTER TWO

I CAN'T LET EVERYONE DOWN. IF MR. MORTON IS RIGHT, WHO KNOWS WHAT MIGHT HAPPEN...

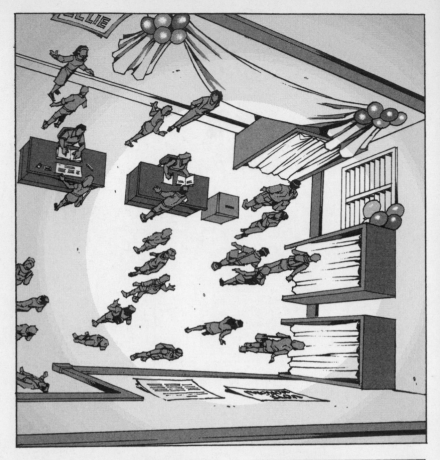

CHAPTER FOUR

CHAPTER FIVE

CONGRATULATIONS, JENNIFER. NOW, AVALON HIGH'S NEW HOMECOMING QUEEN IS...

CHAPTER SIX

For all the books about Ellie and more by

MEG CABOT

check out the following pages!

You'll find:

- Blurbs about Meg's other exciting books
- Info on the Princess Diaries series

Still not enough?
For even more about Meg Cabot, go to:

www.harperteen.com/megcabot

You can read Meg's online diary,
find the latest info on her books,
take quizzes, and get advice
on how to handle the paparazzi.

Ellie has a hunch that nothing is as it seems in

AVALON HIGH

Avalon High seems like a typical school, with typical students. There's Lance, the jock. Jennifer, the cheerleader. And Will, senior class president, quarterback, and all-around good guy. But not everyone at Avalon High is who they appear to be . . . not even, as new student Ellie is about to discover, herself. What part does she play in the drama that is unfolding? What if the chain of coincidences she has pieced together means—like the court of King Arthur—tragedy is fast approaching Avalon High? Worst of all, what if there's nothing she can do about it?

Ellie's story continues in the manga series

Don't miss the thrilling sequels to *Avalon High*:

the mediator

Suze can see ghosts. Which is kind of a pain most of the time, but when Suze moves to California and finds Jesse, the ghost of a nineteenth-century hottie haunting her bedroom, things begin to look up.

Shadowland
Ninth Key
Reunion
Darkest Hour
Haunted
Twilight

1-800-WHERE-R-YOU

Ever since a freakish lightning strike, Jessica Mastriani has had the psychic ability to locate missing people. But her life is anything but easy. If you had the gift, would you use it?

WHEN LIGHTNING STRIKES
CODE NAME CASSANDRA
SAFE HOUSE
SANCTUARY
MISSING YOU

Katie Ellison doesn't mean to be a liar, liar

Pants on Fire

Katie Ellison has everything going for her senior year—a great job, two boyfriends, and a good shot at being crowned Quahog Princess of her small coastal town in Connecticut. So why does Tommy Sullivan have to come back into her life? Sure, they used to be friends, but that was before the huge screwup that turned their whole town against him. Now he's back, and making Katie's perfect life a total disaster. Can the Quahog Princess and the *freak* have anything in common? Could they even be falling for each other?

Is it just bad luck . . . or could it be witchcraft?

Is she just the unluckiest girl on the planet, or could Jean "Jinx" Honeychurch actually be . . . a witch?

Since the day she was born, Jinx has been a lightning rod for bad luck—everything just seems to go wrong when she's around. But she's sure her luck is going to change, now that she's moving to New York City to stay with her aunt, uncle, and super-sweet cousin Tory. Because things can only get better, right? Wrong! Not only is Tory not super-sweet anymore, she thinks she's a witch. She even has a coven of other pretty Upper East Side girls. Jinx is afraid they might hurt someone with their "magic," but she isn't sure how to stop them. Could Jinx's bad luck be the thing that saves the day?

ALL-AMERICAN *Girl*

What if you were going about your average life when all of a sudden, you accidentally saved the president's life? Oops! This is exactly what happens to Samantha Madison while she's busy eating cookies and rummaging through CDs. Suddenly her life as a sophomore in high school, usually spent pining after her older sister's boyfriend or living in the academic shadows of her younger sister's genius, is sent spinning. Now everyone at school—and in the country!—seems to think Sam is some kind of hero. Everyone, that is, except herself. But the number-one reason Samantha Madison's life has gone completely insane is that, on top of all this . . . the president's son just might be in love with her!

Ready OR *Not*

In this sequel to *All-American Girl*, everyone thinks Samantha Madison—who, yes, DID save the president's life—is ready: Her parents think she's ready to learn the value of a dollar by working part-time, her art teacher thinks she's ready for "life drawing" (who knew that would mean "naked people"?!), the president thinks she's ready to make a speech on live TV, and her boyfriend (who just happens to be David, the president's son) seems to think they're ready to take their relationship to the Next Level. . . .

The only person who's not sure Samantha Madison is ready for any of the above is Samantha herself!

READ ALL OF THE BOOKS ABOUT MIA!

The Princess Diaries

THE PRINCESS DIARIES, VOLUME II:
Princess in the Spotlight

THE PRINCESS DIARIES, VOLUME III:
Princess in Love

THE PRINCESS DIARIES, VOLUME IV:
Princess in Waiting

Valentine Princess
A PRINCESS DIARIES BOOK (VOLUME IV AND A QUARTER)

THE PRINCESS DIARIES, VOLUME IV AND A HALF:
Project Princess

THE PRINCESS DIARIES, VOLUME V:
Princess in Pink

THE PRINCESS DIARIES, VOLUME VI:
Princess in Training

The Princess Present:
A PRINCESS DIARIES BOOK (VOLUME VI AND A HALF)

THE PRINCESS DIARIES, VOLUME VII:
Party Princess

Sweet Sixteen Princess:
A PRINCESS DIARIES BOOK (VOLUME VII AND A HALF)

THE PRINCESS DIARIES, VOLUME VIII:
Princess on the Brink

THE PRINCESS DIARIES, VOLUME IX:
Princess Mia

THE PRINCESS DIARIES, VOLUME X:
Forever Princess

ILLUSTRATED BY CHESLEY McLAREN

Princess Lessons:
A PRINCESS DIARIES BOOK

Perfect Princess:
A PRINCESS DIARIES BOOK

Holiday Princess:
A PRINCESS DIARIES BOOK

Girl-next-door Jenny Greenley goes stir-crazy
(or star-crazy?) in Meg Cabot's

TEEN IDOL

Jenny Greenley's good at solving problems—so good she's the school paper's anonymous advice columnist. But when nineteen-year-old screen sensation Luke Striker comes to Jenny's small town to research a role, he creates havoc that even level-headed Jenny isn't sure she can repair . . . especially since she's right in the middle of all of it. Can Jenny, who always manages to be there for everybody else, learn to take her own advice, and find true love at last?

Does Steph have what it takes?

HOW TO BE *Popular*

Everyone wants to be popular—or at least, Stephanie Landry does. Steph's been the least popular girl in her class since a certain cherry Super Big Gulp catastrophe five years earlier. And she's determined to get in with the It Crowd this year—no matter what! After all, Steph's got a secret weapon: an old book called—what else?—*How to Be Popular.*

Turns out . . . it's easy to become popular. What isn't so easy? Staying that way!

But wait!
There's more by Meg:

NICOLA AND THE VISCOUNT

VICTORIA AND THE ROGUE

THE BOY NEXT DOOR

BOY MEETS GIRL

EVERY BOY'S GOT ONE

QUEEN OF BABBLE

QUEEN OF BABBLE IN THE BIG CITY

QUEEN OF BABBLE GETS HITCHED

SIZE 12 IS NOT FAT

SIZE 14 IS NOT FAT EITHER

BIG BONED

INTERVIEW WITH

MEG CABOT'S FUN-FILLED TALE OF MEDIEVAL MAGIC AND SCHOOLYARD DRAMA CONTINUES IN THE AVALON HIGH: CORONATION MANGA! BUT WHO IS THE TALENTED ARTIST THAT BROUGHT THE CHARACTERS YOU LOVE TO LIFE ON PAPER? MEET JINKY CORONADO—VETERAN IN THE WORLD OF COMIC ART AND ARTIST EXTRAORDINAIRE.

Q: COULD YOU FIRST TELL US A LITTLE ABOUT YOUR BACKGROUND? HOW DID YOU KNOW YOU WANTED TO PURSUE A CAREER IN ART?

JINKY: SURE! I WAS BORN AND REARED IN ILOILO, PHILIPPINES. I ATTENDED THE UNIVERSITY OF SAN AUGUSTIN AND GRADUATED WITH A DEGREE IN MARKETING AND A MINOR IN ART. LIFE WAS DIFFICULT...SIX OF US—FATHER PEPITO, MOTHER JUDITH, BROTHERS PEJEE AND JHOPET, SISTER MICHELLE, AND ME—LIVING IN BASICALLY ONE ROOM WITH NO RUNNING WATER. MY DAD WORKED VERY HARD DOING ELECTRONICS REPAIR BUT MADE LESS THAN $2,000 A YEAR IN HIS BEST TIMES. AFTER BEING SELECTED AS "MISS POND'S ASIA" (A PROCESS THAT INVOLVED AN INTERVIEW AS WELL AS OVERALL LOOK—I ENDED UP WITH A LOT OF POND'S PRODUCTS, BUT LATER FOUND I WAS ALLERGIC TO THEM!) AND BEING ON MAGAZINE COVERS, I PAID MY WAY THROUGH SCHOOL BY WINNING BEAUTY PAGEANTS AND MODELING.

I LEARNED HOW TO WRITE AND DRAW COMICS BY ATTENDING THE GLASS HOUSE GRAPHICS CREATING COMICS SEMINARS IN MANILA—A WHOLE BUNCH OF THEM. WHEN I REALIZED I COULD MAKE A REAL LIVING TO SUPPORT MY WHOLE FAMILY BY BOTH DOING COMICS ART AND OCCASIONAL MODELING, I DECIDED TO PURSUE BOTH CAREERS IN THE USA. I STARTED MY SERIES, BANZAI GIRL, AS A SWEET FUNNY SLICE-OF-LIFE PROJECT ABOUT ME IN SCHOOL WITH MY FRIENDS. BUT I WAS LEARNING IN A GROUP THAT CONTAINED GUYS DOING BIG ACTION STORIES—HARVEY (AVENGERS: THE INITIATIVE) TOLIBAO, WILSON (WOLVERINE: THE MANGA) TOROTSA, STEPHEN (WOLVERINE) SEGOVIA, AND SO ON—SO I AMPED UP THE ENERGY BY HAVING MY NAMESAKE MEET VARIOUS FILIPINO MYTHS AND LEGENDS.

I SOLD THE SERIES AT FIRST BY GOING TO CONVENTIONS WEARING THE BANZAI GIRL SCHOOL UNIFORM, SHOWING PAGES, AND GETTING FAN REACTIONS. THE PROPOSAL PACKAGE I SHOPPED AROUND—COMPLETE WITH PHOTOS OF ME IN COSTUME AT THE CONVENTIONS—LED TO THE PHOTO COVERS AND CALENDARS AND SUCH. NOW THE PROJECT IS IN ITS 6TH YEAR OF PUBLICATION!

Q: HOW DID YOU COME TO BE THE ILLUSTRATOR FOR AVALON HIGH: CORONATION?

JINKY: THEY WANTED ME! (LAUGHS) I NEED TO EXPLAIN: BESIDES WRITING AND DRAWING COMICS, I'VE BEEN A MODEL IN PLAY, WIZARD, MIRROR, AND OTHER PUBLICATIONS, PLUS I'VE HAD THREE CALENDARS DEVOTED TO ME. SO, ONE OF THE THINGS I RAN INTO AFTER I CREATED/WROTE/DREW BANZAI GIRL AND THE NEW BANZAI GIRLS SEQUEL FROM ARCANA, WAS PEOPLE REACTING WITH

SURPRISE: "DO YOU REALLY DRAW THIS BOOK?" IT SEEMED AS THOUGH I WAS ALLOWED TO HAVE ONE TALENT—BEING PRETTY—AND NOT ALLOWED TO BE AN ARTIST OR WRITER. PEOPLE SEEMED ASTONISHED I COULD WALK AND CHEW GUM AT THE SAME TIME. (LAUGHS) SO THE APPEALING THING ABOUT AVALON HIGH WAS TO BE ABLE TO DRAW A PROJECT THAT BRINGS SOMEBODY ELSE'S VISION TO LIFE, IN A WAY THAT STILL CONVEYS MY AESTHETIC.

Q: BANZAI GIRLS WAS YOUR OWN CREATION, BUT WITH AVALON HIGH YOU HAD TO DRAW CHARACTERS THAT MEG CABOT HAD CREATED. WHAT SORT OF INSPIRATIONS DID YOU DRAW FROM WHEN CREATING THE CAST?

JINKY: STUDYING PEOPLE. I ALWAYS TURN TO REAL PEOPLE AS MY INSPIRATION. FOR EXAMPLE, THERE'S A CERTAIN BAD GIRL BRUNETTE THAT IS BASED ON MY SISTER, MICHELLE, BECAUSE SHE WAS SO EASY TO "CAST." (SHE'S GONNA WHACK ME WHEN SHE READS THAT.) ALL THOSE FACES AND EXPRESSIONS SHE MAKES COME IN HANDY.

Q: WHO AND WHAT ARE THE EASIEST AND MOST DIFFICULT TO DRAW?

JINKY: BUILDINGS, CARS, HORSES...THEY'RE HARD. PEOPLE ARE EASY. FASHIONS ARE FUN TO DRAW. I LOVE TO DRAW FASHIONS. I'M REALLY INTO SHOPPING FOR CLOTHES AND PURSES AND SHOES, IF THAT GIVES YOU ANY INDICATION. AS FOR THE AVALON HIGH CHARACTERS, YOU MIGHT BE SURPRISED TO KNOW THAT THEY'RE BOTH SUPPORTING CHARACTERS. THE EASIEST ONE WOULD BE MR. MORTON BECAUSE, WELL, WITH THAT THICK BEARD I BASICALLY DRAW ONLY HALF HIS FACE. NOW FOR THE HARDEST, THAT'D BE MRS. WAGNER. SHE'S SO YOUTHFUL AND ATTRACTIVE THAT IT'S EASY TO FORGET SHE'S WILL'S MOM! I ALWAYS HAVE TO MAKE SURE SHE HAS THAT "MOTHERLY" LOOK IN HER FACE.

Q: ASIDE FROM WORKING ON AVALON HIGH, WHAT OTHER EXCITING PROJECTS ARE KEEPING YOU BUSY?

JINKY: BANZAI GIRLS, WHICH IS THE STORY OF ME, AS AN ASIAN SCHOOLGIRL, LIVING LIFE WITH FRIENDS AND FAMILY AND BATTLING FILIPINO MYTHS OR "URBAN LEGENDS"—THE MANANANGGAL, THE DUWENDE, THE KAPRE', THE SNAKE-MAN, THE TIKBALANG, AND SO ON. IT'S FAST BECOME THE ONLY AMERICAN COMIC BOOK SERIES TO REGULARLY FEATURE FILIPINO MONSTERS AND CULTURE. IT'S UNIQUE HERE, BECAUSE AMERICAN MYTHS ARE BASED ON EUROPEAN LEGENDS, AND OURS ARE SO TOTALLY DIFFERENT. THE NEWEST BANZAI GIRLS COLLECTION IS OUT NOW FROM ARCANA STUDIOS, AND AFTER THAT, I HAVE A BRAND-NEW SERIES CONCEPT THAT I HOPE TO BE DOING NEXT YEAR.

Q: WHAT'S YOUR WORK STUDIO (WORKSPACE) LIKE? DO YOU LIKE TO LISTEN TO ANY MUSIC WHILE YOU WORK?

JINKY: I WORK ON A BIG, HEAVY ART TABLE THAT WAS SHIPPED UP FROM BRAZIL FOR ME. I LOVE IT. IT'S BETTER THAN ANY ART TABLE I COULD FIND IN THE U.S. I ALSO HAVE A COMPUTER DESK WITH A LARGE-FORMAT SCANNER, A LARGE-FORMAT PRINTER, AND AN IMAC. I LIKE DANCE MUSIC, FILIPINO MUSIC...SOMETIMES I EVEN HAVE THE TV ON...

Q: THANK YOU SO MUCH, JINKY! DO YOU HAVE ANY LAST COMMENTS FOR YOUR READERS?

JINKY: I HOPE YOU LIKE MY WORK. I'M VERY ACCESSIBLE—CHECK OUT MY WORK ONLINE AND MY MESSAGE BOARD, WHERE I POST RESPONSES AND SHOWCASE PREVIEW ART ALL THE TIME!

THANK YOU ONCE AGAIN, JINKY! FOR YOU FANS OUT THERE INTERESTED IN LEARNING A LITTLE MORE ABOUT HOW AVALON HIGH THE MANGA CAME TO LIFE, FEEL FREE TO SEND ANY FEEDBACK, QUESTIONS, AND COMPLIMENTS TO:

AVALON HIGH FANMAIL
C/O TOKYOPOP
5900 WILSHIRE BLVD., #2000
LOS ANGELES, CA 90036